For Gaëtan Mahé and all traveling children

Orchard Books, A Grolier Company
95 Madison Avenue, New York, NY 10016

Manufactured in France. The text of this book is set in 20 point Bembo Bold.
The illustrations are gouache and acrylic on newspaper.

1 3 5 7 9 10 8 6 4 2

Library of Congress Cataloging-in-Publication Data
Eduar, Gilles.
[Traversée d'Anatole. English]
Dream journey / Gilles Eduar.—lst American ed.
p. cm.
Summary: Jules falls asleep between the humps of Anatole the camel, and the two take a magical dreamtime journey.
ISBN 0-531-30202-4 (trade : alk. paper)
[1. Camels—Fiction. 2. Dreams—Fiction. 3. Stories in rhyme.]
I. Title. PZ8.3.E24Tr 1999 [E]—dc21 99-11728

Dream Journey

Gilles Eduar

Orchard Books • New York

When Anatole the camel reads from his ancient book,

Jules shuts his eyes to listen. He doesn't need to look.

Jules drifts off to sleep, and Anatole sets out.

Who knows where they will go as he starts to walk about.

Anatole begins to swim 'cross the Southern Sea.

Jules is gently lulled by the mermaids' melody.

Through crashing breakers Anatole bravely surfs toward land.

Jules is soothed by waves washing over sand.

Anatole is lost in the jungle east of Quito.

Jules sleeps soundly through the buzzing of mosquitoes.

Anatole rides bravely along a wire from the trees.

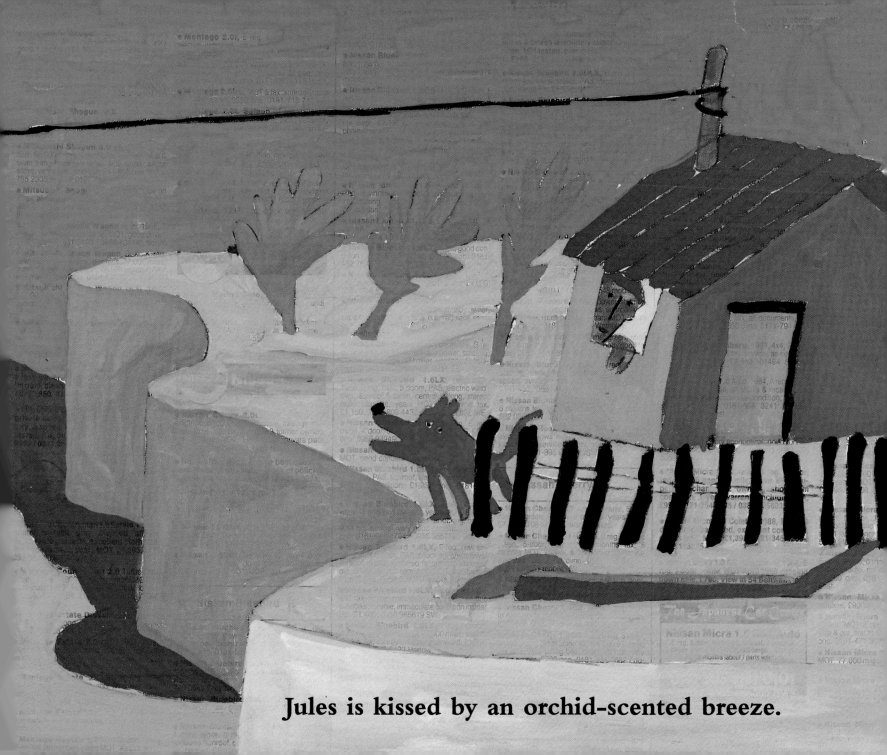

Jules is kissed by an orchid-scented breeze.

On a shiny bicycle, Anatole enjoys a cruise.

Honking horns—*Beep! Beep!*—don't disturb the sleeping Jules.

When lightning strikes close by, Anatole runs—small wonder!

Jules sleeps on through the rolling, rumbling thunder.

Anatole is thrilled to climb the highest mountain peak.

For Jules, a lullaby from the gently flowing creek.

It's cold up north with just a scarf, as Anatole should know.

Jules is blanketed by the softly falling snow.

Anatole is tired as he climbs the final dune.

Jules slumbers on beneath the shining moon.

"Anatole," cries Jules, "I've dreamed of places rarely seen!"

"It's fabulous," says Anatole, "how one can travel in a dream."